CHANGE-A-LOT COOLEST RULEST IN NAPPI

HAMISH HAMILTON/PUFFIN

Published by the Penguin Group
Penguin Books Ltd, 27 Wrights Lane, London W8 5TZ, England
Penguin Books USA Inc., 375 Hudson Street, New York, New York 10014, USA
Penguin Books Australia Ltd, Ringwood, Victoria, Australia
Penguin Books Canada Ltd, 10 Alcorn Avenue, Toronto, Ontario, Canada M4V 3B2
Penguin Books (NZ) Ltd, 182–190 Wairau Road, Auckland 10, New Zealand

Penguin Books Ltd, Registered Offices: Harmondsworth, Middlesex, England

First published by Hamish Hamilton Ltd 1988
1 3 5 7 9 10 8 6 4 2

Published in Puffin Books 1998
1 3 5 7 9 10 8 6 4 2

Copyright © Babette Cole, 1988

Made and printed in Italy by Printer Trento srl

British Library Cataloguing in Publication Data
A CIP catalogue record for this book is available from the British Library

ISBN 0–241–12491–3 Hardback
ISBN 0–140–55527–7 Paperback

King Change-a-lot

by

Babette Cole

PUFFIN BOOKS

Prince Change-a-lot was fed up with being treated like a baby.

His parents, King and Queen Spend-fortune, were making a bad job of running the kingdom and everyone was complaining.

They spent the people's taxes on silly parties and expensive clothes.

They hardly ever saw Prince Change-a-lot, who was looked after by Miss Grumpbladder, the court nanny.

There was a plot to blow up the government offices because nobody was governing properly . . .

and big hairy giants were kicking down
castles left, right and centre . . .

. . . and the bad fairies were cooking up
some rotten spells,

so the good fairies had gone on strike!

To make matters worse, the dragons were
rampaging all over the place,
and flying off with maidens belonging
to the neighbouring kingdoms!

There was a plague of disgusting blubber worms who were eating all the crops.

But the King and Queen
did not want to hear about
anything so distasteful.

Nor did they want to hear about the bad behaviour
in the kingdom's boring old schools.

"I'd change a few things around here,"
said Prince Change-a-lot,
"if only I could talk
like a grown-up."

One day he saw the court magician making
a genie appear by rubbing a pot.
The genie could grant wishes.

The baby genie whizzed over Prince Change-a-lot . . .

BLAH
BLAH
BLAH

. . . and Prince Change-a-lot
started to talk like
the Prime Minister!

The baby genie whizzed over Change-a-lot's parents.

Two minutes later they were behaving like the
worst kinds of babies themselves!

The baby genie whizzed back into the potty.
"OK," said Prince Change-a-lot,
"I'm King now!"

The first thing he did was to give his parents to Nanny Grumpbladder.

Then he turned the government offices into a gigantic fun-fair so that nobody wanted to blow it up.

It had a rubber disco castle for the giants to bounce on, which was far more fun and less painful than kicking down real castles.

King Change-a-lot had all the bad
fairies locked up so that the
good fairies could get back to work.

He gave the dragons video games to play so
that they would stay at home.

The neighbours were pleased to pay the new king for keeping the dragons away.

With the money, he bought lorryloads of cakes and jellies . . .

. . . which he fed to the disgusting blubber worms,
who ate so much jelly they just exploded!

BANG!

SPENDFORTUNE
SCHOOL

CLOSED.

Finally, he closed down all the
boring old schools because he
didn't want to go to one . . .

. . . and he didn't want to send his parents to one either!

King Change-a-lot lived to be a very
clever and popular monarch . . .
. . . with the help of his potty!